To Jack.
~With Love, Julia

That Rule Doesn't Apply to Me!

Written by **Julia Cook**

Illustrated by **Anita DuFalla**

Say **NO** to Rules

BOYS TOWN
Press

Boys Town, Nebraska

That Rule Doesn't Apply to Me!
Text and Illustrations Copyright © 2016 by Father Flanagan's Boys' Home
ISBN 978-1-934490-98-3

Published by the Boys Town Press
13603 Flanagan Blvd.
Boys Town, NE 68010

For a Boys Town Press catalog, call **1-800-282-6657**
or visit our website: **BoysTownPress.org**

Publisher's Cataloging-in-Publication Data

Names: Cook, Julia, 1964- author. | DuFalla, Anita, illustrator.

Title: That rule doesn't apply to me! / written by Julia Cook ; illustrated by Anita DuFalla.

Description: Boys Town, NE : Boys Town Press, [2016] | Series: Responsible me! ; book 3 | Audience: Grades K-6. | Summary: The rules keep getting in the way of Noodle's fun. There are so many rules - too many rules! And Noodle struggles because he doesn't think many of them actually apply to HIM. Will Noodle's mother and teacher convince him that rules are meant to help, not harm, him?--Publisher.

Identifiers: ISBN: 978-1-934490-98-3

Subjects: LCSH: Children--Life skills guides--Juvenile fiction. | Obedience--Juvenile fiction. | Attitude change in children--Juvenile fiction. | Child psychology--Juvenile fiction. | Decision making--Juvenile fiction.
     | CYAC: Conduct of life--Fiction. | Obedience--Fiction. | Rules (Philosophy)--Fiction. | Attitude (Psychology)--Fiction. | Change (Psychology)--Fiction. | Behavior--Fiction.

Classification: LCC: PZ7.C76984 T54 2016 | DDC: [E]--dc23

Personable handwriting: Jack Hughes

Printed in the United States
10 9 8 7 6 5 4

Boys Town Press is the publishing division of Boys Town, a national organization serving children and families.

My name is Norman David Edwards...
but everybody calls me

"Noodle."

Sometimes I get into
trouble because I don't
follow the rules.

But I think there are **way too
many rules** in our world, and some
of them don't even apply to me!

Say
NO
to
Rules

We have...

Rules that say, "You can't eat in here!"
And rules for "Don't pick your nose!"
Rules for people who drive...
Why should I worry about those?

Always use a booger ghost

NO FOOD IN THE COMPUTER ROOM

ONE WAY

YIELD

RIGHT OF WAY

4

At school we have rules for everything...
No hitting, no butting, don't cheat.
Don't run in the halls. You must raise your hand.

"Hey Noodle... Please stay in your seat!"

At home I have a **gazillion rules...**

"No, Noodle, you can't have a pet mouse."

I can't have friends over when
my mom's not home.

And I can't wear my shoes in the house!

I can't have my computer or my video games
in my room overnight.

"It's 10 pm, Noodle, bring your fun
stuff to my room."

"Ah, Mom, that just isn't right!"

We have rules that say, "Brush your teeth twice a day."

And "Put your dishes in the sink."

I have rules for every ounce of my life,
and I think that most of them

STINK!

Yesterday at school when it was time to line up for lunch,
I walked over to stand by my friends in line.

"Teacher... Noodle butted!"

"Noodle, we have a rule for cutting in line,
and you **JUST BROKE THE RULE.**"

"But that rule doesn't apply to me.
I need to stand by these guys, or
I'll end up sitting by girls at lunch!"

"Noodle..."

RATS!
I ended up sitting next to Mary Gold!

You must be 18 years of age

You m̶̶̶ ̶̶̶̶citizen

You̶̶̶ ̶̶̶̶̶residency

r̶̶̶

During social studies, we were having a discussion about elections.

"Why can't kids vote?"
I asked.

"Noodle, we have a rule that says if you want to say something, you need to raise your hand and wait your turn. You just broke the rule because **YOU JUST INTERRUPTED** Reginald."

"Actually, I only bent it and that rule doesn't really apply to me because last week, you told me that I need to get more involved with social studies... so that's what I am doing."

"Noodle..."

RaTS! I had to write a sorry note to Reginald.

Dear Reginald,
    I am sorry that
I interrupted you while you
talking.

During math, I logged onto my fantasy football website to check my score.

"Teacher... Noodle's surfing!"

"Noodle, we have a rule that when we use our tablets for math, the only website you can be on is our district math site, and you just broke the rule!"

"But that rule doesn't really apply to me because I am actually doing math! I'm analyzing my football statistics to see if I can pull out a win!"

"Noodle..."

RaTs!

Now I can't use my tablet in math for TWO WEEKS straight!

Mary Gold has tattle tongue!

FANTASY FOOTBALL

Team Name:
SUPER RAMEN
Round 1-12

Team on

Team t

Then, my day got even worse because my teacher gave us homework in language arts... **my least favorite subject.**

"Class, tonight your assignment will be,
to write a poem from you to me.

Do your best and take your time.
And try to use great words that rhyme.

You get to choose what you put in your poem.
You can start on it now, and finish it at home."

Rats!

When I got home, I ate my snack and headed to my room to work on my poem.

My mom has **this dumb rule** that I have to get all of my **HOMEWORK DONE** before I can play with my friends or play my video games.

I bet I'm the only kid on the planet that has that rule! All of my friends get to do their homework whenever they want, as long as they get it done.

"Noodle, you **CAN'T TAKE YOUR VIDEO GAME** into your room until your homework is finished. You know what the rules are...."

"But that rule doesn't really apply to me, Mom, because my video game isn't even turned on."

"Well, I could agree with you, Noodle, but then we'd both be wrong."

"RATS!"

I sat in my room for about **112 years** trying to figure out what to write... and then I got a really, really great idea!

"I'm done! Can I go play now?"

"Yep, but can you read your poem to me first?"

"Sure!!"

Rules Stink

- a poem by Noodle

Roses are red,
violets are blue.
I wish we didn't have
rules at school!

You cannot run
or jump in the halls.
Be quiet in the library.
Don't write on the walls!

No video games
are allowed at school.
That makes me mad!
I can't stand that rule!

Spit out your gum, Noodle,
at school, you can't chew it.
Show your steps on your math assignment,
so I can see you've worked through it.

Don't push. Don't shove.
Take turns in P.E.
Keep your eyes on your own paper.
Noodle, listen to me!

Be on time, don't be tardy.
And please always share.
Raise your hand, and be patient.
Don't lean back in your chair!

Rules really STINK!
That's all I can say.
It would be SO cool
to have a **Rule-Free Day!**

- The end.

"Noodle, you do realize that having rules is a good thing, don't you?"

"Some rules maybe. But, Mom, I seriously feel like

grown-ups stay up all night thinking up RULES to make my life miserable!"

"Rules aren't made to **HURT YOU,** Noodle, they're made to **PROTECT YOU!** Think about it... if you had a Rule-Free Day at school, it might turn out to **be a disaster!**"

"Your teacher wouldn't know when to start,
because no one would get there on time.
Kids could cut right in front of you,
when you were standing in line.

Whenever you tried to talk,
someone might interrupt you.
Bullying would be OK.
Then what would you do?

Kids could cheat off of your paper
and your teachers wouldn't care.
You might end up
    stepping in somebody's gum.
And someone might
    pull your hair!

You could lean back in your chair if you wanted,
but if you fell, it wouldn't matter.
You wouldn't be able to think in the library,
because there'd be way too much chatter.

Video games would start playing you,
and screen time would take over your life.
Food would get thrown in the lunchroom,
and nothing would feel right.

Everyone could wear what they wanted,
and kids could write on the walls.
School would feel like an unsafe place.
And you wouldn't like it at all!

RULES PROTECT YOU and help you stay organized.
They help you more than you know.
If you didn't have rules in your life,
you couldn't accomplish your goals.

I know you don't like to **FOLLOW THE RULES**,
but I want you to stop and think...
If everyone could do whatever they wanted,
your life would really **STINK!"**

"I guess I've never really thought about it like that," I said.

I went back into my room and fixed my poem (just a little bit), and then I went outside to play.

LANGUAGE
ARTS
ADVERBS

Today, just before school got out, I got to read my poem out loud during language arts.

RULES STINK

a poem by Noodle

Roses are red,

violets are blue,

I wish we didn't have

rules at school!

You cannot run

or jump in the halls.

Be quiet in the library.

Don't write on the walls!

No video games

are allowed at school.

That makes me mad!

I can't stand that rule!

Spit out your gum, Noodle,

at school, you can't chew it.

Show your steps on your

math assignment,

so I can see you've,

worked through it.

$$5(3+7)=x$$
$$(3+7=10)$$
$$5(10)=x$$
$$50=x$$

Don't push. Don't shove.

Take turns in P.E.

Keep your eyes on your own paper.

Noodle, listen to me!

Be on time, don't be tardy.

And please always share.

Raise your hand, and be patient.

Don't lean back in your chair!

Rules really STINK!

That's all I can say.

It would be SO cool

to have a Rule-Free Day!

NOT!

The end

(by Noodle)

"What do you mean by 'NOT!', Noodle?"

"Well, after I thought about it, I realized that **RULES ARE MADE UP TO HELP US,** not hurt us. And, if we had a Rule-Free Day at school, everybody could do whatever they wanted, and school would feel like an unsafe place."

"Excellent answer, Noodle!!!!"

"Class, tonight's homework is to study your spelling words and write two complete sentences for each word."

"We should have a rule that says that teachers can't give kids homework!" I said.

"Noodle... you know how the homework rule works... **ONE SUBJECT A NIGHT FOR 25 MINUTES.**"

"Well, I wish **THAT** rule didn't apply to me!

Homework STINKS!"

Rats!

Getting Kids to Follow the Rules!

Getting children (and adults) to follow rules can be quite a challenge at times. As parents and educators, our job is to keep kids safe, healthy, and happy. To do that, we must teach them to believe in and internalize the importance of following rules.

If you know a child who struggles with following rules, here are a few tips you may find helpful.

1. Remind children that the purpose of rules is to protect us and keep us safe from all harm (physical, emotional, psychological, etc.). If everyone could do whatever they wanted whenever they wanted, the world would be an extremely unsafe place.

2. Involve your child in rule development whenever possible. Explain some rules are non-negotiable (such as safety rules). Others, however, can be negotiated. The more a child can feel in control about developing the rules, the more likely that child will buy into and abide by them. For example, you could allow your child to help create rules for setting up his/her bedtime routine or weekly chore list.

3. Help your child understand that every family and every venue has different rules. Rules at home may be different from rules at school, but all rules should be respected and followed.

4. Provide a framework for basic rules that is repeated often and expected by **ALL**. For example:
- Listen to what Mom, Dad, and your teacher say.
- Always tell the truth.
- Be respectful of others.
- Respect and do no harm to yourself, others, or property.

Remember, children are always watching and learning. Be a good RULE role model!

5. Prior to entering a challenging situation (like dinner at a restaurant), review up to three rule-driven priorities that are expected. For example:
- Let everyone have a chance to speak.
- Use a low or table-talk voice tone.
- Use your best table manners.

6. Catch your child doing something right! The more a child is praised for following rules, the more likely he/she will buy into following them in the future. REMEMBER – It's nice to be noticed when you do the right thing!

7. Whenever possible, institute a natural consequence for not following the rules. For example, if you forget to put your dirty clothes in the hamper, they will not be clean the next time you wish to wear them.

8. It's okay to have conversations with your children about opinions and desires regarding rules. After listening to what your children have to say, empathize with them, yet continue to steer them in the right direction. "I know you love playing with your toys. We can come back later, but right now we need to clean up so we can eat dinner."

9. If a child is constantly pushing limits and refusing to follow rules, take a closer look. The child may not feel recognized or praised enough for doing the right thing, and may be filling his/her need for attention by breaking rules.

10. Set a good example for your child. You can't expect a child to be a rule follower if you are a rule breaker (for example, lying about the age of your children to pay less at a movie, or rolling through a stop sign).

For more parenting information, visit boystown.org/parenting.

Boys Town Press
Books by Julia Cook

Kid-friendly titles to teach social skills

A book series to help kids take responsibility for their behavior.

978-1-934490-30-3

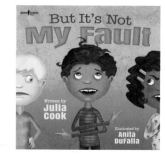

978-1-934490-80-8

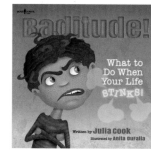

978-1-934490-90-7

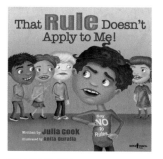

978-1-934490-98-3

978-1-944882-08-2

978-1-944882-09-9

NEW TITLES

Building RELATIONSHIPS

A book series to help kids get along.

Making Friends Is an Art!
Cliques Just Don't Make Cents
Tease Monster
Peer Pressure Gauge
Hygiene...You Stink!
I Want to Be the Only Dog
The Judgmental Flower
Table Talk
Rumor Has It...

COMMUNICATE with Confidence

A book series to help kids master the art of communicating.

Well, I Can Top That!
Decibella
Gas Happens!
The Technology Tail

BEST ME I Can Be!

Reinforce the social skills RJ learns in each book.

The Worst Day of My Life Ever!
el PEOR día de TODA mi vida
I Just Don't Like the Sound of NO!
¡No me gusta cómo se oye NO!
Sorry, I Forgot to Ask!
I Just Want to Do It My Way!
Teamwork Isn't My Thing, and
I Don't Like to Share!
Thanks for the Feedback... (I Think!)
I Can't Believe You Said That!

BoysTownPress.org

For information on Boys Town, its Education Model®, Common Sense Parenting®, and training programs:
boystowntraining.org | boystown.org/parenting
training@BoysTown.org | 1-800-545-5771

For parenting and educational books and other resources:
BoysTownPress.org
btpress@BoysTown.org | 1-800-282-6657